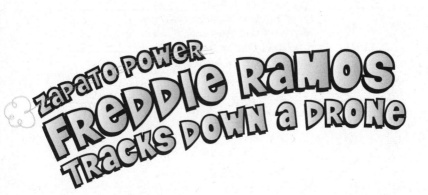

ZAPATO POWER

FREDDIE RAMOS
TRACKS DOWN A DRONE

JACQUELINE JULES   art by MIGUEL BENÍTEZ

albert Whitman & Company
Chicago, Illinois

Don't miss the first eight **Zapato Power** books!

Freddie Ramos Takes Off
Freddie Ramos Springs into Action
Freddie Ramos Zooms to the Rescue
Freddie Ramos Makes a Splash
Freddie Ramos Stomps the Snow
Freddie Ramos Rules New York
Freddie Ramos Hears It All
Freddie Ramos Adds It All Up

Library of Congress Cataloging-in-Publication
data is on file with the publisher.

Text copyright © 2020 by Jacqueline Jules
Illustrations copyright © 2020 by Albert Whitman & Company
Illustrations by Miguel Benítez
Hardcover edition first published in the United States of America
in 2020 by Albert Whitman & Company
Paperback edition first published in the United States of America
in 2020 by Albert Whitman & Company
ISBN 978-0-8075-9563-3 (paperback)
ISBN 978-0-8075-9561-9 (ebook)

Printed in the United States of America
10 9 8 7 6 5 4 3 2 1 LB 24 23 22 21 20

For more information about Albert Whitman & Company,
visit our website at www.albertwhitman.com.

For my editor, Andrea Hall.
Thank you for being Freddie's good friend.
—JJ

Contents

1. A Giant Orange Bug

"What are you making?" my neighbor Maria asked us on Friday afternoon.

She was standing outside the toolshed. Mr. Vaslov and I were inside, working.

"A drone," Mr. Vaslov said. "Come and see."

Mr. Vaslov was an inventor. Most of the stuff he made was top secret, like my super-powered purple sneakers, which go ninety miles an hour and give me super bounce and super hearing.

For a change, we were building something we could talk about.

"Our drone is a flying robot," I told Maria.

"What will it do?" she asked.

That was a good question. Mr. Vaslov had said the drone could help him do his job. He's in charge of taking care of Starwood Park Apartments, where we live. Except I helped Mr. Vaslov when I wasn't in school or playing with my friends. Why did Mr. Vaslov need a drone?

"Let's see!" Mr. Vaslov picked up his project and headed outside.

We watched him set it on the grass and step back with the remote control.

Six spinning blades made the

drone rise into the air.

"Wow!" Maria whistled.

It looked like a giant orange bug and sounded like a race car on a track.

VROOM! VROOM! VROOM!

The drone flew toward Building C.

"No!" Mr. Vaslov called after it. "Stay here."

Inventions are like kids and puppies. They don't always do what grown-ups tell them.

I touched a button on my wristband to turn on my super speed.

ZOOM! ZOOM! ZAPATO!

"Freddie!" Maria called. "Where are you? Wait for me!"

I'm so fast, Maria blinks and I'm gone in a puff of smoke. She and Mr. Vaslov were left way behind.

ZOOM! ZOOM! ZAPATO!

I ran through Starwood Park Apartments, keeping an eye on the big orange bug.

VROOM! VROOM! VROOM!

Mr. Vaslov's drone got lots of attention—just not the good kind.

Mrs. Ramirez opened her window
to complain.

"WHAT'S THAT NOISE?"

The drone hovered near Building
G. Mrs. Ramirez ran out of her
apartment. Her neighbor, Mrs.
Tran, was right behind her,
waving a broom.

"Shoo!" Mrs. Ramirez hollered. "Go away!"

"This is my home!" Mrs. Tran swung her broom like a baseball bat.

Uh-oh! How was I going to stop the neighbors from attacking Mr. Vaslov's drone?

Maria joined me, breathless.

The big orange bug buzzed above us.

"Don't hit it!" she said. "It belongs to Mr. Vaslov!"

Mrs. Tran lowered her broom.

"Hold on! I'm coming!" Mr. Vaslov waved from across

the courtyard.

We waited for him to catch up.

"It's just a robot," Mr. Vaslov said, rubbing his right knee. "It won't hurt you."

"Not true," Mrs. Tran said. "My ears hurt."

"I'm sorry," Mr. Vaslov said. "I need to fix that."

Mr. Vaslov pushed a lever on the remote.

VROOM! VROOM! VROOM!

The giant orange bug zipped away, over the top of Building G.

"Where's it going?" Maria asked.

"I don't know." Mr. Vaslov used

both thumbs to press buttons. "It's out of control."

ZOOM! ZOOM! ZAPATO!

I raced around the corner with my super-powered zapatos. Luckily, not everything Mr. Vaslov makes is so noisy. My shoes hum like one bee in flight, not a whole swarm. And when I zoom by, you only see smoke.

VROOM! VROOM! VROOM!

The big orange bug bumped against a bush and then shot back

into the sky. It bounced off a wall and up to the roof of Building H.

The thing did crazy loop the loops everywhere. I got dizzy just watching it.

And there was no stopping what happened next.

CRASH!

2. Picking Up the Pieces

Maria and Mr. Vaslov hurried over.

"It looks like a plastic pumpkin blew up!" Maria said.

We were lucky she was with us. It took three people to carry the pieces of the dead drone back to the toolshed. And it felt like a funeral.

Mr. Vaslov stood over his worktable, shaking his bushy gray head.

"This is what happens when you hurry," he said. "I should have taken my time and double-checked all the components."

"Components?" Maria asked. "What are they?"

"I'm glad you asked that, Maria." Mr. Vaslov's face brightened. He loved talking about frames, sensors, connectors, and all the other things that went into building his inventions. When he picked up a black rectangle with wires hanging

out of it, I knew Maria was going to get a lesson on the drone's battery pack.

"This powers the motors," Mr. Vaslov explained.

I didn't need to stay. Mr. Vaslov had already taught me about robots and why they needed a power source. Mom would be getting home from work soon. She

expected me
to be at the
kitchen table,
doing my
homework.
    I touched
my wristband and said goodbye.

ZOOM⚡ZOOM⚡ZaPaTO⚡

Mr. Vaslov and Maria were so
busy talking, they didn't even
wave.
    In half a blink, I reached the
sidewalk outside 29G. That's when
I saw a dark blue car with a smiley

face bumper sticker. I'd never seen that car before. But I had seen one of the people inside it: my mom!

What was she doing in a car? Mom took the train home. And who was that man?

I could only see him from the chest up. He wore square black glasses that matched his hair.

And he was smiling with all of his teeth, like his bumper sticker.

Something wasn't right. My mom didn't have a man in her life. My dad was a soldier we lost in the war. We missed him, but we were doing okay, just the two of us.

The man in the blue car was turned sideways, staring into Mom's eyes with a silly look on his face. She was staring back and talking. What was she saying?

I knew I could find out if I turned on my super hearing. Would that be snooping? I tried not to listen to private conversations without a good reason. This sure seemed like one. Mom only had me to protect her.

Just as I was deciding what to do, the car door opened. Mom got out and waved.

"Thanks for the ride home."

"I can't wait for tomorrow," the man said.

Mom giggled. "Me neither."

"Six o'clock?" he asked.

"Six o'clock," Mom repeated.

"I'll be there!" He sounded like someone singing.

They were so loud, I didn't need super hearing to listen. Worse than that, Mom was so busy looking at the man, she didn't even see me standing there, a few feet away on the sidewalk, watching.

"¡*Adiós!*" She waved again and skipped up the walk to our front door.

Little kids skip, not mothers.

This wasn't normal.

The dark blue car drove away.

My stomach felt like a drone had crashed inside.

3. The Man in the Blue Car

"Freddie," Mom said when I walked through the door. *"Mañana va a ser especial."*

"Why?" I asked.

"Tomorrow, a friend is coming for dinner. That makes it special," Mom said.

"The man in the blue car?"

Mom put her hands on her hips. "*¿Cómo lo sabías?*"

"I saw you outside," I explained.

"David is a nice man," Mom said. "I met him at work."

"Is he sick?"

Mom worked in a doctor's office. The people who went there had backaches, sore throats, and other problems.

"No," Mom answered. "He's a drug salesman."

"Drugs!" I shook my head. "How can you like him?"

Mom explained. "David sells medicine. The kind of drugs that make people well."

"Oh," I said. *"Está bien."*

But it didn't feel okay.

Mom took the sugar out of the cabinet. "We will have homemade dessert tomorrow."

Yummy! When Mom had time, she made *arroz con leche.*

"Brownies," Mom added.

"Brownies?" I repeated. "You've never made those before."

"They're David's favorite," Mom said.

What about MY favorite? I liked creamy rice pudding.

Mom got busy with bowls and spoons. She was smiling like the yellow face on the bumper of David's car.

I felt like talking to someone else.

WHEET! WHEET!

My guinea pig, Claude the Second, was happy to see me. And he loved the carrot I had in my hand.

CHOMP! CHOMP!

Claude the Second only needed a treat twice a day to be happy. He didn't have to worry about a man named David who drove a blue car and sold  medicine. Why did Mom like him?

Ding! Dong!

Maria was at the door. She wanted to talk about the drone.

"Mr. Vaslov is going shopping for parts."

"What does he need?" I asked.

"Propellers," Maria said, moving her finger in a circle. "The blades that spin around."

"The new drone will be even better than the old one," I said.

"Yep!" Maria said. "And I'm going to help build it."

"You?" I asked.

Since when did Mr. Vaslov need two helpers?

"Mr. Vaslov says I have a

scientific mind," Maria said.

Really? Mr. Vaslov never told me
I had a scientific mind.

Maria lived in the apartment
next door. We were in the same
class at Starwood Elementary.
We had a lot of the same friends.
Except Mr. Vaslov was *my* friend,
not hers.

"Mr. Vaslov says that drones
can be big or small. They can do
different jobs. Some have crab-
like hands and can carry things.
Some have cameras and can take
pictures," Maria said.

I didn't know that. What else

was Mr. Vaslov telling Maria and not me?

Maria left, and Mom called me into the kitchen. We had microwave macaroni and cheese while the brownies baked.

"Tomorrow night," Mom said, "I'm making lasagna."

"Does David like that too?" I asked.

Mom nodded. "That's what he ordered on our last lunch date."

So Mom had been seeing David

while I was at school. Why didn't she tell me about him before? Was she keeping other secrets from me?

After we ate, I cleared the table so we could play cards. We started off with Go Fish and then moved on to some games my teacher taught me for extra math practice. Playing cards is a lot more fun than doing math problems on a worksheet.

"¡Tú ganas!" Mom threw up her hands. "Four times in a row!"

"Let's make it five," I said, dealing the cards.

Mom winked. "Don't be so sure

you can beat me again."

We played two more games. I had
fun, like I always do with Mom.

But my mind wandered. What if
Mom started spending more time
with David? Would she still play
cards with me on Friday nights?

And what about Maria? Was her
mind scientific? Would Mr. Vaslov
start liking her help more than
mine?

4. Ladybug

The next day, when I knocked on Mr. Vaslov's toolshed, Maria was right beside me.

"Let's get started!" she told Mr. Vaslov.

He was way ahead of us. The broken drone wasn't quite as broken as we'd thought.

"I used carbon fiber," Mr. Vaslov explained. "It's lightweight and durable."

That meant the drone was made out of a really tough material. Most of the pieces just needed to be put back together again.

"Are you making it quieter?" I reminded Mr. Vaslov about Mrs. Tran's broom.

"Yes," Mr. Vaslov said. "The new propellers are bigger, and they spin slower."

Pretty soon, the drone was back in one piece. We hooked it up to Mr. Vaslov's laptop with a cable

that looked like my mom's phone charger.

Mr. Vaslov started typing. "Now we program our drone to tell it what to do."

"Be sure to tell it not to crash," I said.

Mr. Vaslov laughed. "I will."

Maria patted the orange drone. "We should give her a name."

"Okay," Mr. Vaslov said. "What?"

"How about Ladybug?" Maria

said. "She has the same colors—orange and black."

"Good name," I agreed.

Mr. Vaslov checked Ladybug over from top to bottom.

"Let's do a test." He handed Maria a walkie-talkie like security guards use on TV.

"Cool!" she said.

"Can you go to the dumpster and report when the drone lands?"

"Sure thing!" Maria walked away.

It was my turn now. Would I get a walkie-talkie too?

Mr. Vaslov had one left that he kept for himself.

"Your job needs speed," Mr. Vaslov said. "Can you follow the drone and see if it flies straight?"

I stopped feeling jealous. Running was the right job for a kid with super-powered sneakers.

Our big orange bug flew across Starwood Park, just like it was supposed to.

BUZZZZZZZ!

It didn't sound like a race car anymore, just a very big bumblebee.

BUZZZZZZZ!

Ladybug landed on the dumpster outside Building G.

"YAY!" Maria yelled into the walkie-talkie.

"Keep watching!" Mr. Vaslov's voice crackled through the speaker. "I'm sending her back now."

ZOOM⚡ZOOM⚡Zapato⚡

I ran ahead of Maria and followed the drone back to the toolshed. Ladybug flew in a perfectly straight line. Not one loop the loop or crazy bounce.

"What now?" I asked.

"See those crab-like arms?" Mr. Vaslov pointed to the middle of the drone. "Tomorrow, Ladybug will practice carrying things."

"Like what?" Maria asked.

"Pails, tools, boxes," Mr. Vaslov said.

"That's the kind of stuff I carry for you," I said.

Was Mr. Vaslov going to replace

me with a robot?

"True," Mr. Vaslov agreed. "But you're in school during the day, Freddie."

I was still bothered. Why did Mr. Vaslov need more help all of a sudden?

Mr. Vaslov locked the toolshed, and we turned to walk home just as Maria's younger brother, Gio, came rushing over with Puppy, his little dog.

"Guess what I saw!"

Gio thinks it's his job to tell everybody what he sees.

"What?" I asked.

"A man just walked into Freddie's house," Gio said.

Dinner! I'd been so busy with the drone, I'd forgotten that David was coming at six.

"He's my mom's friend," I said.

"Is he nice?" Maria asked.

"I don't know," I answered. "I haven't met him."

"He'd better be," Mr. Vaslov said. "Freddie's mom deserves the best."

The crashed drone feeling came back to my stomach. What if David wasn't good for my mom? Or me?

"Freddie's mom could get

married," Maria said. "He could get a new dad."

Uncle Jorge in New York is going to be Juanita's dad when he gets married. I'll get a new cousin. But we've all known each other for a while now.

"Don't get ahead of yourself," Mr. Vaslov said. "First, we have to meet this guy."

Mr. Vaslov had a good idea. If my friends met David, they could help me decide if he was okay.

"Will you come home with me?" I asked.

5. David

"Freddie!" Mom said. "You brought your friends!"

Her voice was really high. I don't think she expected me to walk in with Mr. Vaslov, Maria, and Gio.

"Yes," I answered. "They wanted to meet your friend."

Everyone turned toward David, who was standing by the couch

with a roll of candies in his hand. He had just popped one in his mouth when Gio charged at him.

"Peppermints!" he said. "Can I have one?"

"Sure!" David dropped a round, white candy into Gio's hand and then walked toward Maria and me. "Would you like one too?"

Maria took a peppermint. I shook my head. If you take candy from someone, it means you trust them.

After Mom introduced me to David, Mr. Vaslov introduced himself.

"I'm not Rosa's father," he told David. "But she feels like a daughter to me."

Did that mean Mr. Vaslov cared for me like a grandson? Maybe I didn't have to worry about being replaced by a robot after all.

"You want to make sure I'm not a bad guy," David answered.

Wow! How did he know what I

was thinking?

When they finished their candy, Maria and Gio went home to their own apartment for dinner. Mr. Vaslov stayed to eat with us.

For a while, it was great. Mr. Vaslov talked to David so I didn't have to.

"What are your hobbies, David?"

"Photography," he said. "I like cameras and taking pictures."

"Really?" Mr. Vaslov's eyes widened behind his glasses.

That started a conversation on lenses, light sensors, and other electronic stuff.

I didn't have to say a thing until David looked right at me.

"What do you like to do, Freddie?"

That was a hard question. My favorite thing was zooming around in my super-powered zapatos. After that, I liked using my super bounce and super hearing. How could I talk about that? Only Mr. Vaslov knew I had superpowers, because he invented them.

"Freddie?" Mom prodded me. "David asked you something."

"Uh." I stared down at my lasagna. "I don't know."

"Then tell me what you did today, Freddie," David said.

At least that question was easy to answer.

"I helped Mr. Vaslov build a drone."

"You have a drone?" David asked Mr. Vaslov. "I just bought one with a camera."

"Is it a quadcopter?" Mr. Vaslov asked. "With four arms?"

"Yes," David answered. "I call her Birdie."

"Bring her over tomorrow," Mr. Vaslov said. "Birdie can meet our Ladybug."

Sunday morning, David was back
at Starwood Park, showing off a
green drone half
the size of Ladybug.

"Let's see them
fly," Mr. Vaslov
said.

We stood in the big grassy area
beside Building G, where I liked to
play soccer.

Mom was with us. She held her
hands over her heart, watching the
two drones in the sky. One flew on
the left side, the other on the right.

"¡Increíble!" she said.

Then things went wrong. Birdie veered toward Ladybug.

"I'm sorry!" David pushed the buttons on his remote. "I lost the signal for a moment."

"Sometimes there's radio interference," Mr. Vaslov said, "from power lines or other wireless signals in the air."

BUZZ! BUZZ! BUZZ!

Birdie went too close again.

"I'll send Ladybug higher," Mr. Vaslov said, "out of Birdie's way."

That didn't work so well. Ladybug disappeared.

David brought Birdie down,

and we all moved in different directions, looking for Mr. Vaslov's orange drone. I was the fastest.

ZOOM! ZOOM! ZaPaTO!

I circled all the buildings. Ladybug wasn't anywhere on the ground at Starwood Park.

Was she still flying? I turned on my super hearing to hear noises from far away.

All I heard was a little kid crying because his sister took his toy car. No buzzing drone sounds.

ZOOM! ZOOM! ZAPATO!

Superheroes don't quit. I kept running with my eyes peeled—up, down, everywhere.

On the other side of Building H, I finally spotted something orange in a tree. Could I get a closer look?

Sure! I had super bounce.

BOING! BOING! BOING!

Yep! Ladybug was there, waiting to be rescued.

6. Learning to Fly

BOING! BOING! BOING!

Super bounce is super handy. I didn't need a ladder. One quick grab and Ladybug was out of the tree, only a little bit bent.

"Freddie!" Mom ran over with David right beside her.

"You found Ladybug," he said. "You're a hero!"

Hero! My favorite word! Should I be happy, hearing it from David?

We took Ladybug to the toolshed and showed her to Mr. Vaslov.

"Please let me help fix her," David said. "It's my fault."

"Thanks." Mr. Vaslov put Ladybug on his worktable. "But I'll have to do it later. Mrs. Lopez has a dripping faucet."

Mr. Vaslov walked away from us toward Building C.

"He's limping," I said, "like his leg hurts."

Mom sighed. "Mr. Vaslov is having trouble with his knees.

Many older people do."

Is that why Mr. Vaslov wanted Ladybug? Could a drone help him? Wouldn't it be better if he had something to ride around on?

I didn't have much time to think about that before David asked me a question.

"Would you like to fly Birdie?"

Who could say no to that?

David handed me a controller

with a cell phone attached.

"You two have fun!" Mom waved. "I have some laundry to do."

Flying a drone meant learning what the levers and buttons were for. It wasn't as easy as I thought it would be.

"Push the stick gently," David said. "Make the drone rise slowly."

We practiced hovering and landing softly. Then David taught me how to go forward and backward, right and left. Pretty soon, the drone was doing exactly what I wanted it to.

"That's it, Freddie," David said.

"Smooth and steady."

Maria came by and looked over my shoulder. She liked watching the screen on the remote. Birdie had a camera, and we could see the view from above Starwood Park.

"It's what you would see if you were a bird, flying," David said.

"Can I try?" Maria asked.

She caught on quickly, but she didn't push the stick quite as gently as David wanted. Birdie soared over Building F.

"Hold on," David said, taking the controls. "We need to bring her back into our line of sight."

But Birdie didn't want to come. The camera showed her flying lower and lower.

"What's happening?" Maria asked.

David shook his head. "It's the battery. I should have switched to a fresh one."

"She's falling!" Maria pointed at the screen.

We watched Birdie tumble to the ground.

"I'll get her," Maria offered.

"No," I said. "I'm faster! Let me!"

ZOOM! ZOOM! zapato!

With super speed, it only took
half a blink to run around Building
F, pick up Birdie, and return.

ZOOM! ZOOM! Zapato!

"Oh no!" Maria cried. "One of
the propellers broke."

David narrowed his eyes. I was
almost glad to see it. He'd been

way too friendly. Now he was going to show us who he really was and get mad over the broken drone.

But I was wrong. Something else was bothering David.

"What just happened, Freddie?" he asked. "Did you step out of a puff of smoke?"

RATS! I'd made a BIG mistake. Zooming off was not smart. Maria was so used to it, she'd stopped asking questions. David was another story.

"Ummm," I mumbled. "Ummm."

The back of my neck felt hot. What was I going to say?

Maria saved me.

"Freddie does that." She waved her hand. "He's just real fast."

David opened his mouth so wide, I could see his back teeth.

I was glad when Mr. Vaslov came across the grass and interrupted us.

"What's going on?" he asked.

David showed him the broken propeller.

"Looks like we have two drones to fix," Mr. Vaslov said. "Come to my toolshed."

When Mr. Vaslov and David walked off together, Maria turned to me.

"Everybody likes your mom's new boyfriend," she said.

Was everybody right? Should I like David too?

I needed more time to make up my mind.

7. Looking for Clues

Maria had flying fever. On Monday, it was all she could talk about.

"Do you think Mr. Vaslov will let us fly Ladybug?"

"If he can watch," I said, "and if we promise to be careful."

After school, we knocked on the toolshed door.

"Sorry, kids," he said. "My drone is missing."

"What happened?" Maria asked.

"I took her out for another test," Mr. Vaslov answered. "She got away from me again."

"Which way did she go?" Maria asked.

Mr. Vaslov pointed toward Building C. "I searched until my knee gave out."

"It's okay," I told Mr. Vaslov. "We'll get her back."

"I hope so," Mr. Vaslov said. "But drones are very popular."

"You think somebody took her?"

I asked.

Mr. Vaslov shrugged. "You never know."

"Let's split up," I told Maria. "You check this side of Starwood Park. I'll check the other."

ZOOM⚡ZOOM⚡zapato⚡

I circled Starwood Park twice. No Ladybug.

Maybe she was in a tree again.

BOING! BOING! BOING!

I checked every tree around. No Ladybug.

Where was Mr. Vaslov's drone?

I needed more clues. Maybe someone had seen it. Or maybe someone had hit it with a broom.

I knocked on Mrs. Tran's door.

"Yes," she said. "I saw that orange monster by the dumpster."

ZOOM! ZOOM! ZaPaTO!

I raced over there, but all I found was a roll of peppermint candy— the same kind David had handed out on Saturday night. Was he here?

While I was thinking, Gio walked over with Puppy. "Guess what? David brought your mom

home."

"How do you know?" I asked.

"I saw them get out of the blue car with the smiley face sticker."

So David was at Starwood Park.

"Did you see anything else?" I asked Gio.

"Just before he left, David put something orange in the trunk of his car."

Ladybug was orange. Did David take her? How could I find out?

I raced home to talk to Mom.

"Can we go to David's house?" I asked.

She answered me with a sneeze. "*Achoo!*"

"Sorry, Freddie," she said. "I have a cold."

"Can we still go?"

"*Achoo!*" Mom sneezed again. "Where?"

"To David's house. He saw our house. We should see his."

Mom smiled. "So you like David?"

"I didn't say that. I said I wanted to see where he lives."

"*Muy bien.*" Mom smiled again. "I'll ask him about Saturday night."

"Can't we go sooner?" I asked.

"*Achoo!*" Mom sneezed. "I need to get well first."

I sighed. Five days was a long time to wonder if my mom was dating a thief.

On Saturday night, we took the train to a tall building downtown. We had to go through a lobby, up an elevator, and down a hallway to reach David's door.

"Welcome!" he said as we walked inside.

The table was set with a red tablecloth and white dishes.

"We're having *pupusas*," David said. "I found a recipe on the internet."

I remembered how Mom had made lasagna for David. Was this how grown-ups showed they liked each other? They cooked their favorite foods?

At dinner, Mom and David told me about how they met.

"I knew David's face," Mom said. "He has meetings at my office."

"But we didn't talk until the day Mr. Torrez dropped his cane," David said.

"And you helped him." Mom smiled.

Mom thought David was the kind of person who helped others. What if David was really the kind of person who took other people's drones?

"May I use the bathroom?" I asked.

"Sure," David said. "It's at the end of the hall."

David's bedroom door was wide open. I only had to take a little peek to see what was inside. Uh-oh!

I saw a table in the corner of the room with a few tools and a big orange drone.

8. The New Project

David sure made it easy for me to catch him. A smart crook would have hidden the drone in the closet, not left it out for anyone to see.

I went back to the table, not knowing what to do. Should I tell Mom? Or wait until I could talk to Mr. Vaslov?

"You're frowning, Freddie," Mom said. "Are you feeling all right?"

"Not really," I said. Mom put her hand on my forehead. "Maybe you're coming down with my cold."

Since we'd already finished dessert, Mom decided we had to go home. David took us in his blue car.

"*Gracias*," Mom said as we got in and she buckled her seat belt. "You're very sweet."

"So are you," David said.

"Dinner was wonderful," Mom said.

I sat in the backseat, listening to Mom and David talk, until we reached Starwood Park and passed Mr. Vaslov's toolshed.

"The lights are on!" I said.

"Mr. Vaslov must be working late," Mom said.

What was he building? A new drone to replace the one David took?

Mr. Vaslov liked David. Mom did too. How could the two people I trusted most in the world be so wrong?

It wasn't easy to sleep that night. My head was too full of questions. And in the morning, I dreamed about an orange drone buzzing outside my window.

Tap! Tap!

I opened my eyes. Was it Ladybug? No. It was Gio.

"Get dressed, Freddie," Gio said through the glass. "Mr. Vaslov needs help."

"What happened?"

"Nothing," Gio said. "He just wants you."

Gio was better at telling than explaining.

ZOOM⚡ZOOM⚡ZAPATO⚡

I rushed outside to find Mr. Vaslov on Mrs. Tran's stoop, rubbing his knee.

"Can you go to the toolshed? I need a light bulb."

ZOOM! ZOOM! ZAPATO!

I was back in a blink.

"Thank you, Freddie." Mr. Vaslov
stood up. "Now Mrs. Tran will
have light in her bathroom."

I was glad Mrs. Tran didn't have to
do her business in the dark anymore.
But I wasn't happy Mr. Vaslov was
having trouble with his leg.

"I'm going to the doctor next
week," Mr. Vaslov said.

"I hope it helps," I said.

"If it doesn't," Mr. Vaslov
grinned, "I have a new project that
will."

"Can I see?"

After he replaced the lightbulb, we walked to the toolshed. The new project was a red electric scooter.

"This should help more than a drone," I said.

"Absolutely," Mr. Vaslov said. "With this scooter, I should have no more problems with going back

for tools or light bulbs."

Mr. Vaslov didn't want the drone anymore. Should I forget what I saw in David's apartment?

¡Claro que no! Mom and Mr. Vaslov had to be told.

I took a deep breath and forced the words out. "David has Ladybug."

"I know," Mr. Vaslov answered.

What? Mr. Vaslov knew?

"David found her by the dumpster on Monday," Mr. Vaslov said, "and called me."

That still didn't explain why I saw Ladybug in David's apartment.

Why didn't he give the drone back right away?

"David put a camera on Ladybug," Mr. Vaslov said. "Now I'll be able to check the roofs with my drone. I won't have to climb ladders."

"That's really nice," I said.

"David is thoughtful," Mr. Vaslov said. "He could be good for your mother."

But would he be good for me? I could only find out if I gave him a chance.

A few minutes later, David parked his blue car at Starwood

Park and came walking toward us. He had the orange drone in his arms.

Mom came over too. She was carrying a cooler.

"Who wants to go on a picnic?" she asked.

"No thanks," Mr. Vaslov said. "I have a scooter to finish."

"I'll go." I raised my hand like I do in school when I want to be picked.

David drove us to a park outside the city.

"This is a better place to fly," David said. "Lots of wide open space."

After lunch, David sat on a blanket with Mom, while I flew Birdie.

BUZZ! BUZZ! BUZZ!

She soared in perfect circles above our heads.

Don't Miss Freddie's Other Adventures!

One day Freddie Ramos comes home from school and finds a strange box just for him. What's inside?

HC 978-0-8075-9480-3
PB 978-0-8075-9479-7

In this sequel, Freddie has shoes that give him super speed. It's hard to be a superhero and a regular kid at the same time, especially when your shoes give you even more power!

PB 978-0-8075-9483-4

Freddie's super-speedy adventures continue— now he has superhero duties at school!

PB 978-0-8075-9484-1

When Freddie's zapatos go missing, how can he use his zapato power?

HC 978-0-8075-9485-8
PB 978-0-8075-9486-5

There's a blizzard in Starwood Park—but the weather can't stop a thief! It's up to Freddie and his Zapato Power to save the day!

HC 978-0-8075-9487-2
PB 978-0-8075-9496-4

What happens when Freddie outgrows his zapatos?

HC 978-0-8075-9497-1
PB 978-0-8075-9499-5

How will Freddie
learn to use his new
super hearing without
becoming a super snoop?

HC 978-0-8075-9500-8
PB 978-0-8075-9542-8

Freddie's failing math and
trying to protect a new
girl at school—but his
Zapato Power is no help!
What will Freddie do?

HC 978-0-8075-9539-8
PB 978-0-8075-9559-6

Jacqueline Jules is the author of more than forty books, including *Freddie Ramos Takes Off*, a Cybils Award winner. She lives in northern Virginia, just outside Washington, DC. Visit her at www.jacquelinejules.com.

Miguel Benítez likes to describe himself as a "part-time daydreamer and a full-time doodler." He lives with his wife and two children in England.